THE SNOW QUEEN

Written by Saviour Pirotta
Illustrated by Lucy Fleming

Once upon a time, a long, long time ago, an evil snow
queen owned a horrible mirror. Everything reflected
in it, no matter how beautiful, looked hideous.

Quarto is the authority on a wide range of topics.

Quarto educates, entertains and enriches the lives of our readers—enthusiasts and lovers of hands-on living.

www.quartoknows.com

Author: Saviour Pirotta
Illustrator: Lucy Fleming
Designer: Victoria Kimonidou
Editor: Ellie Brough

© 2017 Quarto Publishing plc
First published in paperback in 2019 by QED Publishing,
an imprint of The Quarto Group.
T (0)20 7700 6700 F (0)20 7700 8066
www.QuartoKnows.com

A catalogue record for this book is available from the British Library.

ISBN 978 0 7112 4452 8

Manufactured in Shenzhen, China PP082019

9 8 7 6 5 4 3 2 1

But one day, the mirror broke and
it shattered into a million fragments.

The wind scattered the fragments
to all corners of the world.
A tiny sliver of glass fell
into a window box
full of roses.

It lay there, hidden,
until one summer...

"Ouch," said Kai, who was
watering the roses with his
best friend Gerda. "There's
something in my eye."

The glass instantly froze Kai's heart. Everything he saw now looked nasty and horrible.

In a rage, he tore the roses
to shreds. Gerda, who loved all
living things, was heartbroken.

Winter came and Kai was still angry with
the world. One day, while he was out
riding his sledge, he saw a sleigh.

He was tired, so he decided
to hitch his sledge to it.

He did not know that it was the Snow Queen's sleigh.
"Sit beside me," she said, smiling a cool smile.
And with that, Kai was under her spell.

The Snow Queen's sleigh swooped up high into the sky,
carrying Kai far from home.

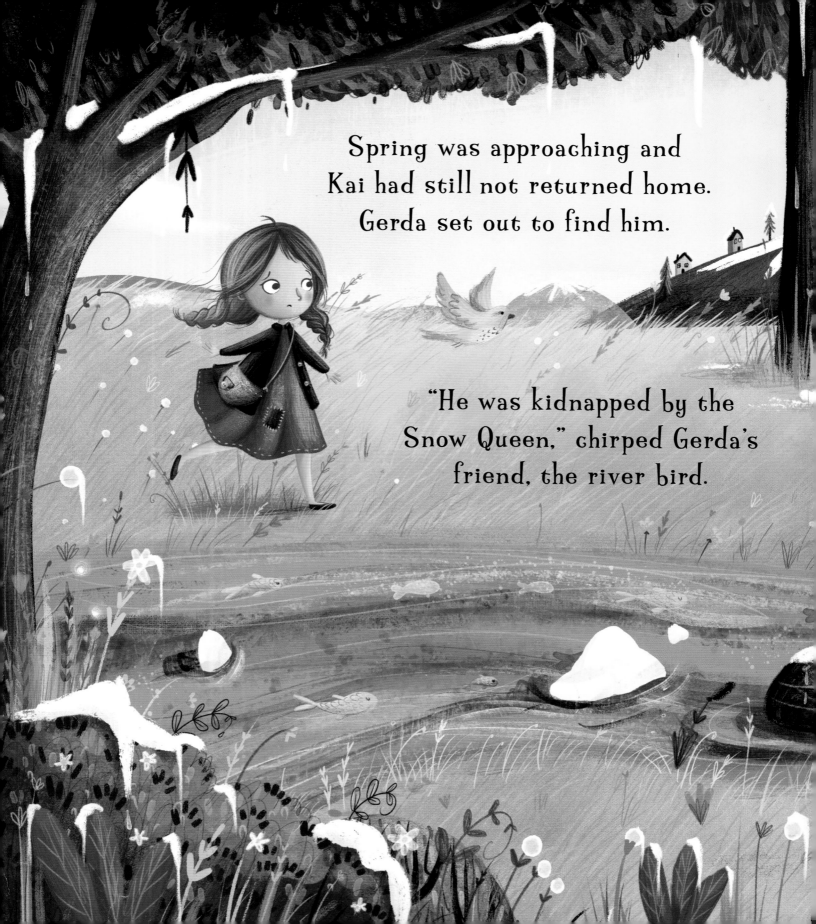

Spring was approaching and
Kai had still not returned home.
Gerda set out to find him.

"He was kidnapped by the
Snow Queen," chirped Gerda's
friend, the river bird.

"I shall find a boat and
sail to the Snow Queen's
palace," said Gerda.

Soon Gerda came to a summer
island where a witch lived.

"Why don't you stay?"
said the witch, offering
Gerda a cherry.

One bite of the
ripe fruit, and Gerda
forgot all about Kai.

But later, she woke
up from the spell
and remembered.

She returned to
her boat and set off
again to find Kai.

Away she sailed, up rivers and far across seas, getting colder and colder until the boat got stuck in the ice.

"How shall I get to the Snow Queen's palace now?" exclaimed Gerda loudly.

"You can borrow Bae, my reindeer," said a girl who was fishing nearby.

Bae carried Gerda to the Snow
Queen's palace. The Snow Queen was
away but she had left Kai behind.

"I've come to
take you home,"
cried Gerda.

Kai looked puzzled.
He did not recognise Gerda.

Saddened, Gerda kissed him and her
tears warmed Kai's heart. The sliver
of mirror fell from his eye.

"Gerda? Is it you?" Kai exclaimed. "Where are we?"
Gerda's tears turned to joy at Kai's words.

Kai looked puzzled.
He did not recognise Gerda.

Saddened, Gerda kissed him and her
tears warmed Kai's heart. The sliver
of mirror fell from his eye.

"Gerda? Is it you?" Kai exclaimed. "Where are we?"
Gerda's tears turned to joy at Kai's words.

danger," she said

"Let's go home before the
Snow Queen returns."

New roses bloomed in the window box. Kai thought they were the most precious things in the world.

Next Steps

Discussion and comprehension

Ask the children the following questions and discuss their answers:

· Can you find a picture that shows you it is: Spring/Summer/Winter? What are the clues?

· What happened to make Kai change from a nice boy to being angry with the world?

· Why couldn't Gerda continue her journey in the boat?

· Can you find some words that describe the Snow Queen?

Activity

Gerda and Kai were best friends. Ask the children to think of the things that make a good friend and write them down. Ask the children specifically what made Gerda a good friend in the story? Give the children a piece of paper and ask them to illustrate their best friend. Ask them to write a sentence to say what they are doing in the picture that makes them a good friend.

Create a window box of roses

Give the children brown card, green paper and red tissue paper, scissors and glue or sticky tape. Ask them to make a window box of roses like in the story. Give them some silver foil so that they can make the shard of glass to put in too.